The Weather Fairies Collection

Volume 1: Books #1-4

Crystal the Snow Fairy
Abigail the Breeze Fairy
Pearl the Cloud Fairy
Goldie the Sunshine Fairy

by Daisy Meadows

SCHOLASTIC INC.

New York   Toronto   London   Auckland
Sydney   Mexico City   New Dehli   Hong Kong

ISBN-13: 978-0-545-10631-3
ISBN-10: 0-545-10631-1

Weather Fairies #1: *Crystal the Snow Fairy*, ISBN-10: 0-439-81387-5,
Text copyright © 2004 by Rainbow Magic Limited.
Illustrations copyright © 2004 by Georgie Ripper.

Weather Fairies #2: *Abigail the Breeze Fairy*, ISBN-10: 0-439-81386-7,
Text copyright © 2004 by Rainbow Magic Limited.
Illustrations copyright © 2004 by Georgie Ripper.

Weather Fairies #3: *Pearl the Cloud Fairy*, ISBN-10: 0-439-81388-3,
Text copyright © 2004 by Rainbow Magic Limited.
Illustrations copyright © 2004 by Georgie Ripper.

Weather Fairies #4: *Goldie the Sunshine Fairy*, ISBN-10: 0-439-81389-1,
Text copyright © 2004 by Rainbow Magic Limited.
Illustrations copyright © 2004 by Georgie Ripper.

12 11 10 9 8 7 6 5 4 3   13 14/0

Printed in the U.S.A.   40

First Scholastic Printing, October 2009

Contents

Crystal the Snow Fairy   1

Abigail the Breeze Fairy   73

Pearl the Cloud Fairy   143

Goldie the Sunshine Fairy   215

The Fairyland Palace

Forest

Candy Factory

The Village Hall

River

Wetherbury Village

Far

Jack Frost's
Ice Castle

een Wood

Mrs. Fordham's House

The Park

Willow Hill

High St.

The
Museum

rsty's
ouse

Fields

Mudhole

N
W E
S

Goblins green and goblins small,
I cast this spell to make you tall.
As high as the palace you shall grow.
My icy magic makes it so.

Then steal the rooster's magic feathers,
Used by the fairies to make all weathers.
Climate chaos I have planned
On Earth, and here, in Fairyland!

Crystal
the Snow
Fairy

For my friend, Joe Heaney,
who has always been
magical to me!

Special thanks to
Narinder Dhami

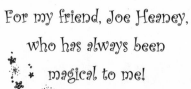

A Magical Surprise

"Isn't it a beautiful day, Mom?" Kirsty Tate asked happily. She gazed out of the car window at the blue sky and sunshine. "Do you think it will stay like this for all of summer vacation?"

Mrs. Tate laughed. "Well, let's hope so," she said. "But remember what the weather

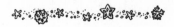

was like on Rainspell Island? It was
always changing!"

Kirsty smiled to herself. She and her
parents had been to Rainspell Island for
vacation during the last school break.
Kirsty had made a new friend there,
Rachel Walker, and the two girls now
shared a very special secret. They were
friends with the fairies! When evil Jack
Frost had put a spell on the seven
Rainbow Fairies and banished them
from Fairyland, Rachel and Kirsty had
helped the fairy sisters get back home.

"Could Rachel come and stay with us
for a little while, Mom? Please?" Kirsty
asked, as they pulled up outside their
house. The Tates lived in Wetherbury, a
pretty village in the middle of the
countryside.

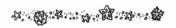

"That's a really good idea," Mrs. Tate agreed. "Now, let's take this stuff inside."

"OK," said Kirsty, climbing out of the car. "Where's Dad?"

Just then, a voice called out from the distance. "Hello, I'm up here!"

Kirsty glanced up, shading her eyes against the sun. To the left of the house was an old wooden barn. Mr. Tate was standing at the top of a ladder next to the barn, holding a hammer.

"I'm just repairing the barn roof," he explained. "It's been leaking."

"Oh, dear," said Mrs. Tate, opening the car trunk. She handed two shopping bags to Kirsty. "We really have to do something about that barn. It's falling down."

"I like it," Kirsty replied. Suddenly, she jumped. Something cold and wet had landed on her nose! "Oh, no!" she exclaimed. "I think it's raining." Then she stared at the white flakes that had landed on her pink shirt. "It's not rain," she gasped. "It's *snow*!"

"Snow?" Mrs. Tate looked shocked. "In summer? It can't be!"

But it *was* snowing. In a flash, the sky had turned gray and snowflakes were floating down.

"Quick, Kirsty, let's get inside!" called Mrs. Tate, grabbing the rest of the shopping bags and closing the trunk of the car.

Mr. Tate was already climbing down from the ladder. They all rushed inside as the snow swirled around them.

"This is very strange," said Mr. Tate, frowning. "I wonder how long it will last?"

Kirsty glanced out of the kitchen window. "Mom, Dad, the snow stopped already!" she cried.

Mr. and Mrs. Tate joined Kirsty at the window. The sun was shining and the sky was blue. A few puddles of water were all that remained of the sudden snowstorm.

"Well!" said Mr. Tate. "How strange! It was almost like magic!"

Kirsty's heart began to pound. Could there be magic in the air? But why? She and Rachel had found all of the Rainbow Fairies, and Jack Frost had promised not to harm them again. Everything was fine in Fairyland now, wasn't it?

"You'd better go and change out of that wet shirt, Kirsty," said her mom.

Kirsty turned away from the window.

As she did, she spotted something on the kitchen table. It was a rusty old metal weather vane in the shape of a rooster. "What's that?" she asked.

"I found it in the park this morning," her father said. "It will look great on top of the barn once I'm done fixing the roof."

Kirsty reached a hand toward the weather vane. As she did, the metal glowed, and glittering sparkles danced toward her fingers. Kirsty blinked in surprise. When she looked again, the sparkles had vanished. All she could see was the rusty metal.

Confused, Kirsty ran upstairs to change. Had she imagined the sparkles? Maybe. The snow was real, though. She was sure of that. "I'll call Rachel after lunch," she thought. "Maybe she's been noticing strange things, too."

Kirsty hurried into her bedroom. There, on a shelf above her bed, was the snow globe the fairies had given her. It was a very special thank-you gift for helping the Rainbow Fairies. Rachel had one, too. It was filled with glittering fairy dust, in all the colors of the rainbow. When the snow globe was shaken up, the dust swirled and sparkled inside.

Right now, no one was shaking the
snow globe — but the fairy dust was
swirling around inside the glass! Kirsty
forgot about her wet shirt and kept
staring at the sparkling snow globe. She
couldn't believe her eyes. "It must
be magic!" she whispered.

She ran across the room and
grabbed the glass globe,
but then dropped
it with a gasp
of pain. The
snow globe
was so hot it had
burned her fingers!

As the globe fell, it hit
the edge of the shelf and
shattered.

"Oh no!" Kirsty exclaimed, upset

that she'd broken her beautiful gift. Just
then, sparkling fairy dust flew into the
air, and floated down around her. Before
she knew it, Kirsty was shrinking! It was
just like on Rainspell Island. She and
Rachel had become fairy-size when they
helped rescue the Rainbow Fairies. Now
she was tiny all over again!

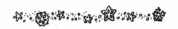

Kirsty twisted around to look over her shoulder. There were her fairy wings, delicate and glittering. "Maybe the fairies want me to fly to Fairyland to see them," Kirsty said to herself. "But I don't know how to get there!"

As she spoke, the fairy dust drifted around her. Suddenly, a strong breeze swept in through the open window. It picked up the fairy dust and whipped it into a whirlwind of glitter. Then, the whirlwind lifted Kirsty gently into the air and carried her right out the window!

Trouble in Fairyland

Kirsty was whisked through the sky in a whirl of colorful fairy dust. She flew over rivers, mountains, trees, and houses, passing fluffy white clouds on the way. Soon, she saw the red-and-white toadstool houses of Fairyland below her. There was the river, winding its way

through the green hills. The water
sparkled like diamonds in the golden
sunshine.

The wind was
bringing Kirsty down
now, close to the silver
Fairy Palace and its pretty
pink towers. Kirsty
could see King
Oberon and
Queen Titania
waiting for her
with a group of
fairies. And
next to the queen
was someone else
that Kirsty knew
very well.

"Rachel!" called Kirsty.

Rachel rushed over as Kirsty
landed gently on the grass.
"I came the same way you did,"
Rachel explained
excitedly, giving
Kirsty a hug.
"My snow
globe broke,
and the fairy
dust brought me
here."
"Do you
know why?"
asked
Kirsty.
Rachel shook
her head as the
king and queen
and their fairies joined the girls.

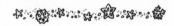

"It's wonderful to see you both," said Queen Titania, smiling. "But I'm afraid we need your help again," she added, looking worried.

"I hope you don't mind us bringing you here like this," King Oberon said.

"Of course not!" Kirsty said eagerly. "Is something wrong?"

The queen sighed. "I'm afraid that Jack Frost is up to his old tricks again."

Rachel looked shocked. "But he promised not to harm the Rainbow Fairies anymore!" she said, glancing up at the sky with a shiver. The sun had disappeared, and it had turned suddenly chilly.

"That's true," Queen Titania replied. "Unfortunately, he didn't promise not to harm our Weather Fairies!" She waved

18

her hand at the seven fairies standing
nearby.

"You mean this strange weather is all
because of Jack Frost?" asked Kirsty, as
sunshine broke through the gray clouds
again.

The queen nodded. "Doodle, our
weather vane rooster, is in charge of
Fairyland's weather," she explained.
"Doodle's tail is made up of seven

beautiful feathers. Each feather controls one kind of weather."

"Every morning, Doodle decides on the best weather for every part of Fairyland," the king went on. "Then he gives each Weather Fairy the correct feather, and they go off to do their weather work."

Rachel and Kirsty were listening hard.

"Come with us," said the queen. "We'll show you what's happened."

The king and queen led Rachel and Kirsty into the palace gardens and over to a golden pond.

The queen scattered some fairy dust onto the water, and it began to fizz and bubble.

After a moment, the water grew still and clear. A picture began to appear on the surface. It showed a beautiful rooster with a magnificent tail of red, gold, and copper-colored feathers.

"That's Doodle," the queen explained. "Yesterday morning he

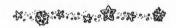

planned the weather for Fairyland, like
he always does."

Rachel and Kirsty watched
as Doodle flew to the top
of the palace and perched
on one of the pink towers.
He spun slowly around,
gazing out over the hills of
Fairyland. Then he nodded
his feathery head and flew down again.

"Jack Frost has always helped Doodle
and our Weather Fairies with the winter
weather," the king continued. "There's
so much work, with all the ice and snow
and frost. But now it's summer, and Jack
Frost has nothing to do."

"So he's bored," the queen put in.
"And that means trouble! Look. . . ." She

pointed at the pictures appearing on the water.

Doodle was standing on the palace steps, waiting for the Weather Fairies to collect their feathers.

Kirsty gasped. "Look, Rachel!" she cried. "The goblins!"

Rachel remembered the goblins. They were Jack Frost's servants, and they were mean and selfish. They had big feet, pointed noses, and ugly faces.

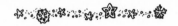

Seven goblins were creeping toward Doodle. The rooster did not see them until it was too late. The goblins reached out and snatched Doodle's tail feathers. Then, they ran away with the feathers, laughing as they went.

"Oh no!" said Kirsty, as the rooster chased after the goblins. "Poor Doodle!"

"It gets worse." The queen sighed. "The goblins escaped into the human world, and Doodle followed them. And now Doodle is very far away from Fairyland, and without his magic tail feathers, his powers just won't work," she explained.

"Doodle turned into an ordinary metal weather vane," the king said sadly. "We don't even know where he is now."

"We need you to find the goblins," the queen said. "It's the only way to get Doodle's tail feathers back. Until then, Doodle is stuck in your world, and our weather will be all mixed up!" She looked up at the sky as a few raindrops began to fall. "The goblins are causing weather trouble for humans, too."

"Our Weather Fairies will help you," the king told the girls. "Let me introduce

you. This is Crystal the Snow Fairy, Abigail the Breeze Fairy, Pearl the Cloud Fairy, Goldie the Sunshine Fairy, Evie the Mist Fairy, Storm the Lightning Fairy, and Hayley the Rain Fairy."

The fairies gathered around Rachel and Kirsty. "Pleased to meet you!" they cried in sweet voices. "Thank you for helping us!"

"Each Weather Fairy will help you find her own feather," said the queen. "And we know the goblins are hiding somewhere here. . . ."

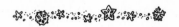

She sprinkled more fairy dust over the water, and the picture changed. Now, Rachel and Kirsty could see a pretty town surrounded by lush green fields.

"Oh!" Kirsty exclaimed. "That's Wetherbury! That's where I live. So *that's* why we had the snowstorm. It was the goblins!"

"What snowstorm?" asked Rachel.

Kirsty quickly explained. "And I think I know where Doodle is, too," she went on eagerly. "I think he's the rusty old weather vane my dad found in the park!"

A Snowy
Start

"Thank goodness Doodle is safe!" cried
Queen Titania happily.

"But the snowstorm means that one of
the goblins is close to your town," the
king warned. "And he must have
Doodle's magic Snow Feather!"

Kirsty turned to Rachel. "Do you think
your parents will let you come and stay

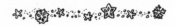

with me?" she said. "My mom said it was OK."

"I'll ask them," Rachel replied. "Then we can get the feathers back from the goblins!"

The king nodded. "That would be wonderful," he said.

The queen stepped forward. She had two golden lockets in her hand. "Each locket is filled with fairy dust," she explained, giving them to the girls. "You can use a pinch of this whenever you need to turn yourself into fairies and back

into humans again. But remember!" She smiled at Rachel and Kirsty. "Don't look too hard for magic — it will find you. And when it does, you will know that one of the magic feathers is close by."

The girls fastened the lockets around their necks.

"And beware of the goblins," the king added. "Jack Frost has cast a spell to make them bigger than usual."

"Bigger!" Rachel said, feeling nervous. "As big as humans, you mean?"

31

The king shook his head. "We have a law in Fairyland that not even magic can make anything bigger than the highest tower of the Fairy Palace." He pointed at the tallest pink tower. "But it means that now the goblins are almost as tall as your shoulders — when you're human-sized."

Kirsty shivered. "We'll have to be careful," she said. "But of course we're happy to help."

Rachel nodded.

"Thank you," said the king gratefully. "We knew you wouldn't let us down."

The queen scattered fairy dust over the girls. It whipped around them, and in a few seconds, a whirlwind was gently lifting them up into the sky.

"Good-bye!" Kirsty and Rachel called,

waving at their friends below. "And
don't worry. We'll find Doodle's feathers
and bring him safely home."

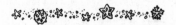

"Rachel's here!" Kirsty shouted, rushing
to the front door.

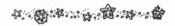

The Walkers' car was just turning in to the driveway.

"Put on your boots before you go out in the snow," called Mrs. Tate from the kitchen. Kirsty pulled on her boots. It was the day after she and Rachel had been to Fairyland, and Rachel's parents had agreed that she could come and stay with the Tates. Kirsty had been worried that the Walkers wouldn't be able to make it to Wetherbury, though. The goblins had been up to their tricks again.

There had been a heavy snowfall, and flakes were still drifting down.

Kirsty ran outside, followed by her mom and dad. The Walkers were unloading Rachel's suitcase from the car.

"Hello," called Mr. Tate. "Sorry about the weather. Isn't it awful?"

"I packed my boots, scarf, and gloves in my suitcase," Rachel whispered to Kirsty as they hugged hello.

"Would you like to come in for some coffee?" Mrs. Tate asked.

"That would be nice," Rachel's mom agreed. "But we shouldn't stay too long, in case the snow gets worse."

"Come and see Doodle," Kirsty said quietly to Rachel, as their parents chatted.

Mr. Tate had put Doodle inside the hall closet. Gently, Kirsty lifted the weather vane out.

"Oh, poor Doodle!" said Rachel when she saw the rusty rooster. "We have to find his feathers, Kirsty!"

A knock at the front door made them both turn.

"I wonder who that is?" Kirsty said, putting Doodle away again.

Kirsty's mom had opened the door and

was talking to an old lady who was bundled up in winter clothes.

"It's Mom's friend, Mrs. Fordham," Kirsty whispered to Rachel. "She lives on Willow Hill."

"I'm sorry to bother you," Mrs. Fordham was saying, "but there's so much snow, I can't get back to my house. I wondered if I could wait here for a while."

"Of course," said Mrs. Tate, helping her inside. "Come and have a cup of coffee.

"I've never seen weather like this,"
Mrs. Fordham went on, unwinding her
scarf. "And it seems to be worse on
Willow Hill than anywhere else. I don't
know why."

Kirsty and Rachel glanced at each
other.

"Why do you think there's more snow
on Willow Hill?" Rachel whispered to
Kirsty.

Kirsty looked excited. "Maybe that's
where the goblin has taken the Snow
Feather!"

"Let's go and find out," Rachel
suggested.

Kirsty ran to ask her mom if she and Rachel could go out to play in the snow. Meanwhile, Rachel quickly changed out of her summer clothes. The girls said good-bye to their parents and hurried outside. It was still snowing.

"Quick," said Kirsty. "We have to make it to Willow Hill before the goblin gets away."

"Wait for me!" called a tiny voice behind them.

The Grouchy Goblin

Kirsty and Rachel spun around.

A tiny fairy with crystal-colored wings
was sliding down the gutter pipe. She
wore a soft blue dress with fluffy white
edging. Her wand was tipped with silver,
and her hair was in pigtails.

"Look! It's Crystal the Snow Fairy!"
Kirsty gasped.

The girls rushed over to her.
"Hello again!" Crystal
called. She looked
excited. Tiny,
sparkling snowflakes
fizzed from the tip
of her wand. "Look
at all this snow,"
Rachel said.
"We think your
feather is close by."
"So do I," agreed
Crystal. "I can't wait to
find it! But there must be a goblin
nearby, too. . . ." She shivered, and her
wings drooped. "We have to be careful."
"We're going to Willow Hill," Kirsty
explained. We think the feather may be
over there."

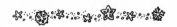

Crystal fluttered down and landed on Rachel's shoulder. "Let's go!" she cried.

They headed out of the Tates' garden and walked up Twisty Lane onto High Street. There were lots of people around, so Crystal hid inside a fold of Rachel's scarf.

Crowds of children were playing in
the park, throwing snowballs and
building snowmen. They were having
fun, but the snow was causing lots of
problems, too. The girls passed a few cars
that were stuck in snowdrifts. There were
other cars that had broken down. A
broken pipe at the post office had
flooded the road, and some of the shops
were closed.

"How much farther is Willow Hill?"
Rachel panted. It was hard work,
tramping through the deep snow.

Kirsty pointed up ahead of them.
"There it is," she replied breathlessly.

Rachel's heart sank. The snow-covered
hill looked very high. As they trudged
out of the village, the snow seemed to be
getting deeper, too. It was almost up to
the top of Rachel's boots.

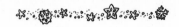

"I have an idea," Kirsty said suddenly, as her feet sank into a snowdrift. "Why don't we use some of our fairy dust? Then we can fly the rest of the way!"

Crystal popped her head out of Rachel's scarf. "Good idea!" she said.

Kirsty and Rachel opened their lockets. They each took a pinch of fairy dust and sprinkled it over themselves. Immediately, they began to shrink, and wings grew from their shoulders.

"Come on." Crystal took their hands. "Let's fly to the top of the hill. I can see a house up there."

"That's Willow Cottage," explained Kirsty. "It's Mrs. Fordham's house."

Crystal and the girls flew to the top of the hill, dodging the falling snowflakes, which seemed as big as dinner plates to Rachel and Kirsty.

As they got closer to the cottage, Kirsty spotted smoke coming from the chimney. "That's funny!" she said with a frown. "Mrs. Fordham lives by herself,

and she's at our house. So who started
the fire?"

"Let's look inside," suggested Crystal.

The three girls swooped down and
hovered outside a frosty window. Crystal
waved her wand to melt some of the
frost, making a small peephole. They
peered inside.

Sitting on the floor, in front of a roaring fire, was a big goblin. And in his hand was a shimmering copper feather, spotted with snowy-white dots.

Crystal gasped. "The Snow Feather!" she whispered excitedly.

A Sneaky Plan

As Kirsty, Rachel, and Crystal watched, the goblin sneezed loudly.

"A-CCCH-O-O-O!" When the goblin sneezed, a shower of ice cubes clattered to the floor. They began to melt, leaving behind little puddles of water.

"The goblin doesn't know how to use the magic feather properly," Crystal whispered.

Kirsty and Rachel were a little frightened. Because of Jack Frost's spell, the goblin was now pretty big. He looked very scary with his mean face, pointed ears, and big, flat feet.

The goblin huddled closer to the fire. He was grumbling and rubbing his toes. "I'm so cold," he moaned. "And my feet hurt!"

Crystal smiled. "Goblins hate to have cold feet!" she murmured.

"How are we going to get the feather back?" asked Kirsty.

"Let's fly around the house and look for a way in," Rachel suggested.

They flew around, checking all the windows and doors. But everything was locked. They could still hear the goblin muttering about his cold feet.

Kirsty grinned. "I have an idea!" she said. "Dad just decided to give away a pair of slippers that were too small for him. If I wrap them up in a box, I can deliver the package to the goblin.

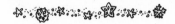

Then he'll open the door for us, and we can get inside."

"Perfect!" Crystal agreed, as her wand fizzed sparkly snowflakes. "The goblin won't be able to resist a present. And if Rachel and I hide inside the box, maybe we can get the feather back."

Quickly, they all flew back to the Tates' house. With a wave of her wand, Crystal turned Kirsty human-size again. Then she and Rachel hid inside Kirsty's pockets.

Kirsty let herself quietly into the house and found the slippers, which her dad had put in a pile to give away. Then she wrapped the slippers in lots of tissue paper and put them in a shoe box.

"You can come out now," she whispered to Crystal and Rachel. Luckily, all the parents were chatting with Mrs. Fordham in the living room, and hadn't heard a thing.

Crystal and Rachel flew into

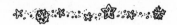

the shoe box and hid under the tissue
paper.

Kirsty popped the lid back on the box
and wrapped it neatly in brown paper.
Then she set off again for Willow Hill.
She couldn't fly up the hill with the
package, so she had to walk.

By the time she reached Willow
Cottage, Kirsty was out of breath and wet
with snow. "We're here," she said quietly

to Crystal and Rachel.
Then she took a deep
breath, knocked on the
door, and waited.
There was no reply.
Kirsty knocked again.
"Delivery!" she called.
"Go away!" the
goblin shouted.

Kirsty tried
again. "Some nice
warm slippers for
Mr. Goblin!"
she said loudly.

This time the
door opened, just a
crack. Kirsty held
the package

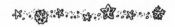

out. The door opened wider, and a bony hand shot out and grabbed the box.

Then the door was slammed shut in Kirsty's face. Kirsty hurried to the window and peeked in. The goblin was tearing the paper off the shoe box. He pulled out the slippers, popped them on his feet, and stomped around the room to try them out. They were a bit big, but he looked delighted. He settled down happily in a chair by the fire, stretched out his feet to

admire the slippers, and fell fast asleep.
The shining Snow Feather lay on his lap.

Kirsty watched as the tissue paper in
the box began to move. Crystal and
Rachel fluttered out.

Crystal flew over to the snoring goblin
and lifted the feather from his lap.

"You'd better make me human-size again, Crystal," Rachel whispered. "Then I can open the window and we can escape."

Crystal nodded. She waved her wand over Rachel, who instantly shot up to

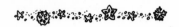

her full size. Then Rachel unlatched the window and pushed it open.

An icy blast of wind swept into the room.

"What's going on?" the goblin roared, jumping up from his armchair.

A Very Unusual Snowball

"Quick!" Kirsty gasped, pulling Rachel through the window.

Crystal flew out too, her face pale with fear.

The goblin spotted the Snow Fairy and gave another furious roar. He ran over to the window, jumped out, and followed the girls.

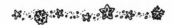

Kirsty and Rachel hurried down the hill. It was hard to run fast because the snow was so deep.

"Hurry!" Crystal called. She was flying above them, the feather in her hand. "He's getting closer!"

Rachel glanced anxiously over her shoulder. The goblin was catching up!

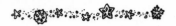

But then she saw him fall over in his too-big slippers. Yelling loudly, he rolled head over heels down the hill, picking up snow as he went.

"Watch out, Kirsty!" Rachel gasped. "The goblin's turned into a giant snowball!"

The goblin's arms and legs stuck out of the snowball as it rolled down the hill. Quickly, the girls dove out of the way. The snowball shot past them and rolled away, faster and faster. Soon it was out of sight.

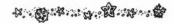

"Are you all right?" asked Crystal, flying over to her friends.

The girls were picking themselves up and brushing snow from their clothes.

"We're fine!" Kirsty beamed. "But can you stop the Snow Feather's magic?"

Crystal nodded and expertly waved the Snow Feather in a complicated pattern. Immediately, the snow clouds vanished. Overhead, the sky was blue and the sun shone. By the time the girls made their way back to the Tates' house, the snow had melted away.

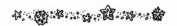

As Kirsty and Rachel walked into the house, with Crystal safely hidden in Kirsty's pocket, Mrs. Tate smiled.

"Hello, girls," she said. "Isn't it funny how the weather's changed? Your mom and dad have gone home, Rachel. At least they won't have to worry about the snow now. I hope it stays nice for the rest of your visit."

Kirsty and Rachel grinned at each other.

"Your dad's in the garden, Kirsty," Mrs. Tate went on. "He's attaching that old weather vane to the barn roof."

Kirsty and Rachel ran outside. They looked up on top of the barn — and there was Doodle! Mr. Tate was busy in his shed, so he wasn't watching.

"Quick, Crystal." Kirsty took the Snow Fairy out of her pocket. "Give Doodle his tail feather back!"

Crystal nodded. Fluttering her shiny wings, she flew up to Doodle and put the big tail feather into place.

The girls gasped in surprise as copper and gold sparkles fizzed and flew from Doodle's tail. The iron weather vane vanished. In its place was Doodle, just as colorful as he had been in Fairyland!

Doodle turned his head and stared straight at Kirsty and Rachel. "Beware!" he squawked. But before he could say

any more, his feathers began to stiffen
and he became metal again.

"What was he trying to say?" Rachel
asked, puzzled.

Kirsty shook her head. She had no idea.

"I don't know either," sighed Crystal.

"But it must be important. What if he was trying to warn us about other goblins?"

Kirsty frowned. "Maybe he'll be able to tell us more when we bring back his other feathers."

"Yes," Crystal agreed. She waved at Rachel and Kirsty. "And now that you've found the Snow Feather, I have to return to Fairyland. The king and queen will be so happy. Good-bye, and thank you!"

"Good-bye!" Rachel and Kirsty called.

The girls waved as Crystal flew up into the sky, her wings glittering in the sun.

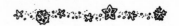

Kirsty turned to Rachel. "And now we have only six more magic feathers to find," she said.

Rachel nodded. "I wonder where the next one will be!"

Rachel and Kirsty looked at the sunny sky and wondered what adventure — and weather — the next week would bring.

Abigail
the Breeze
Fairy

Dedicated to the real fairies who
make my garden grow.

Special thanks to
Sue Bentley

The Adventure Begins

"I'm so glad I could come and stay with you!" Rachel Walker said happily. She sat with her friend, Kirsty Tate, in the garden outside Kirsty's house. The sun shone brightly on the green lawn and pretty flowering bushes.

"Me too," agreed Kirsty, smiling. "And it's very exciting to help the fairies again!"

Kirsty and Rachel had met while on vacation with their parents a few months earlier, and they'd had a wonderful fairy adventure. Jack Frost had cast a nasty spell to banish the seven Rainbow Fairies from Fairyland, and the girls had helped rescue them. With Rachel and Kirsty's help, the fairies were able to bring color back to Fairyland!

Now Jack Frost was causing even more trouble in Fairyland. He had ordered his goblin servants to steal the seven magic feathers from Doodle, the weather vane rooster. Doodle and the seven Weather Fairies were in charge of the weather in Fairyland. But without his magic tail feathers the rooster was powerless! Fairyland's weather would be all mixed up until Rachel and Kirsty could help the

Weather Fairies find all seven of Doodle's stolen feathers.

"I hope we find another magic feather today," said Rachel. She and Kirsty had already helped Crystal the Snow Fairy return the Snow Feather to Doodle.

The goblins were hiding all around Wetherbury, where Kirsty lived. And they had been up to lots of mischief, using the magic feathers to create some very unusual weather in the country village.

Kirsty looked anxious. "We still need to find six more feathers," she said. "Or poor Doodle will be stuck on top of our barn forever!" She glanced up at the roof of the old

wooden barn. Here in the human world, the magical rooster was just a rusty metal weather vane.

Just then, a bush near the garden gate began to rustle. Kirsty and Rachel could see its pink flowers jiggling. "Do you think there's a goblin in that bush?" Kirsty whispered.

"Yes! I can see it moving." Rachel gasped. She was worried about facing another goblin. They were much scarier now that Jack Frost had cast a spell to make them bigger.

"Come on!" Kirsty said, running across the lawn. "He might have one of Doodle's feathers."

Rachel followed her, watching the bush nervously.

An angry screech came from the middle of the bush. Rachel and Kirsty looked at each other in surprise. Suddenly, two cats shot out and chased each other into the barn.

"Oh!" Kirsty exclaimed, and she and Rachel laughed with relief.

Just then, Kirsty's mom appeared at the front door. "There you are, Kirsty," she said. "Would you and Rachel like to go to the Summer Festival in the village? You can cheer your grandma on in the Cake Competition. She's hoping to win this year."

Kirsty and Rachel looked at each other and smiled. "We'd love to," Kirsty replied. "Gran makes the best cakes!"

Mrs. Tate laughed. "Yes, she does. But you'd better hurry if you want to get there before the judging starts."

A few minutes later, the girls were hurrying down Twisty Lane toward High Street. It was a beautiful day. Birds soared in the blue sky and wildflowers dotted the bushes like tiny jewels. As they walked by a thatched cottage with a pretty garden full of roses, a sharp gust of wind blew a shower of flower petals onto the sidewalk.

Just then, a large white envelope landed at Kirsty's feet. "Where did that come from?" she murmured, and then she gasped as more letters came spinning and whirling toward her.

"The wind's really blowing hard now," Rachel said, stooping to pick up some of the letters.

"Hey! Come back!" called a voice. A mailman was running toward them, chasing the envelopes that had been carried away by the breeze.

The girls picked up the letters from the ground and handed them to the mailman. He grinned and stuffed them back into his bag.

"Thanks," he said. "This wind's really strong. Listen, it's even blowing the church bell now!"

He walked on to deliver his letters as Kirsty and Rachel hurried toward the festival. As they walked, they could hear the church bell clanging in the breeze.

The wind seemed to be getting stronger
and stronger. When the girls arrived at
the festival, they saw that the wind
was causing chaos there. Strings of flags
had come loose and were blowing in the
wind like kite tails. Three tents strained
against their ropes as they billowed and
swayed. Many of the stallholders had to

fight to stop their goods from blowing
away.

With a loud snap, the side of a tent tore
free from its ropes and began flapping in
the wind. Some men ran over to tie it
back down. "I've never seen wind like
this in the middle of summer," one of
them complained.

As the girls headed off to look for the Cake Competition, Kirsty noticed a small boy struggling to hold on to a yellow balloon. Suddenly, the wind whipped it out of his hand.

"My balloon!" cried the boy.

"We'll catch it!" called Kirsty, already running after the balloon.

Rachel followed her friend. "There's something very strange about this wind!" she shouted.

"I know," puffed Kirsty, jumping up to catch the balloon's string. "Do you think it could be magic?"

The girls looked at each other, their eyes shining with excitement.

Cake Chaos!

Kirsty and Rachel caught the balloon
and took it back to the little boy, who
was standing outside one of the tents.
When he saw it, the boy's face lit up.
"My balloon!" He beamed. "Thank you."
  "You're welcome," Kirsty replied.
  Just then, she heard a familiar voice.

"Hello, Kirsty," called a plump, jolly-looking lady, as she hurried over to join the girls.

"Hi, Gran," Kirsty said. She turned to Rachel. "This is my dad's mom, Grandma Tate," she explained.

"Hello, Mrs. Tate," said Rachel. She glanced at the huge cake tin that Kirsty's gran held in her hands. "Is that the cake you're entering in the competition?"

Kirsty's gran nodded. "It's a chocolate fudge cake," she said. "That grumpy Mrs. Adelstrop always wins the competition. But I think I have a chance this year."

"Who's Mrs. Adelstrop?" Rachel asked.

Just then, another woman with a cake tin pushed by. "Out of my way!" she demanded. "This wind is terrible!" With that, she disappeared inside a nearby tent.

"I'll bet you've guessed who that was," whispered Kirsty's gran.

"Mrs. Adelstrop!" the girls replied.

"You got it right on the first try," said Gran with a laugh. "Well, I have to go get ready now. See you girls soon!" And she followed Mrs. Adelstrop into the tent.

"Good luck," called Rachel.

"Should we go inside, too?" Kirsty asked. "The goblin with the Breeze Feather must be close by. He might even be hiding inside the tent."

Rachel nodded and the girls wandered into the tent. A tall, thin man with a notepad stood behind a table full of

delicious-looking cakes. Mrs. Adelstrop smiled confidently and placed an enormous lemon cake on the table.

"That looks pretty good," Kirsty whispered, noticing the sugared lemon slices on top.

But then Kirsty's gran took out her chocolate fudge cake. Layers of chocolate sponge and buttercream filling were topped with icing and chocolate leaves. Mrs. Adelstrop's smile faded when she saw it.

"Wow! That's Gran's best cake ever!" Kirsty exclaimed happily.

"It looks delicious," Rachel agreed.

But as Mrs. Tate stepped forward to place her cake on the table, a huge gust of wind blew in through the entrance of the tent. A colored rope covered with flags snaked into the tent and wrapped itself around her legs.

Mrs. Tate stumbled, and the cake flew out of her hands. It sailed through the air and landed — *splat* — right in the judge's face!

Kirsty's gran looked horrified.
"Oh, how awful! Look at that poor
judge," she whispered to the girls.
"And there go my chances of winning
the Cake Competition this year!" she
added sadly.

"What an awful accident," said Mrs.
Adelstrop loudly. Kirsty could tell she was
trying not to look happy.

The judge stood there, covered in chocolate icing, as everyone rushed to help him clean up. The sound of the howling wind surrounded the tent, and the canvas flapped loudly.

"The wind's getting worse," whispered Rachel. "Let's see if the goblin is hiding under the table."

Kirsty lifted a corner of the tablecloth and peeked underneath, but there was no sign of a goblin.

Rachel glanced around the tent, looking for other possible goblin hiding places. Her eyes fell on a pretty fairy decoration, perched on top of a cake. Suddenly, she gasped. The tiny fairy was waving at her!

Goblin Discovered

The fairy's bright green eyes sparkled with laughter. She wore a pretty yellow top and a matching skirt with a little green leaf on it. Her long brown hair was tangled and windswept, and she held an emerald-green wand with a shining golden tip. Little bursts of golden leaves swirled from the tip of her wand.

Rachel's eyes widened. "Kirsty! Over here!" she whispered.

Kirsty hurried over. "It's Abigail the Breeze Fairy," she said happily. She and Rachel had met Abigail and all the other Weather Fairies in Fairyland.

"Hello, Rachel and Kirsty!" Abigail said, smiling. She twirled in the air in a cloud of gold-green dust and tiny bronze leaves.

"Thank goodness we've found you," said Rachel. "We think there's a goblin nearby."

Abigail's tiny face paled. "Goblins are nasty things — so big and scary! But we have to find this one," she said bravely, "before he causes any more trouble with the Breeze Feather." She fluttered her glittering wings and swooped onto Rachel's shoulder to hide underneath her hair.

"Well, the goblin isn't in this tent," said Kirsty. "Let's go outside and check the booths."

"Good idea," Rachel agreed, and the two friends left the tent, struggling against the blustery wind. They hadn't gotten far when they heard a loud creaking noise. Suddenly, the tent behind them collapsed! The girls saw Kirsty's gran rushing to help others, who were crawling out from beneath the canvas.

"Oh, what a mess!" said Rachel.

"At least it doesn't look like anyone's hurt," Kirsty pointed out.

The wind moaned loudly through a group of oak trees nearby. The branches thrashed back and forth, and green leaves rained down.

Abigail's tiny mouth drooped. "Poor trees. It's too soon for them to lose their leaves," she said sadly.

"This is more goblin mischief!" fumed Kirsty. "If that goblin keeps using the Breeze Feather, he'll tear the leaves off all the trees."

Quickly, the girls searched the tents and some of the stalls, but they didn't have any luck at all finding the goblin — or the Breeze Feather.

Then, Kirsty heard a dog barking. "It's Twiglet," she said, pointing at a cute

Jack Russell puppy next to the raffle booth. "His owner is one of our neighbors, Mr. McDougall."

"We haven't searched the raffle booth yet," Rachel said. "Let's go and check there for goblins."

The girls hurried over. "Hello," Kirsty greeted her neighbor.

"Hello, my dear," said Mr. McDougall. "I don't think Twiglet likes this windstorm."

Kirsty nodded. She bent down to pet
Twiglet, and the puppy jumped up from
beside his empty food bowl. He wagged
his tail and wiggled his little nose. Kirsty
stroked his soft, floppy ears. "You're
gorgeous," she said,
smiling.

"What's that?"
Rachel asked,
pointing to a torn
piece of material in
Twiglet's mouth.

Kirsty pulled the
material away from Twiglet. It was
brown leather and it smelled moldy.

Rachel and Kirsty looked at it closely.

"I'm sure I've seen something like this
before," Rachel said thoughtfully. "I
wonder where Twiglet got it."

Suddenly, Twiglet began barking again. He was staring up at the sky, and jumping up and down.

"That's odd," said Mr. McDougall. "He keeps doing that. I wonder why."

"Maybe he's hungry?" suggested Rachel.

Mr. McDougall shook his head. "Can't be. His dish is empty. He must have eaten all of his food when I wasn't looking."

Twiglet snapped and growled, still looking upward. The girls and Abigail followed the puppy's gaze toward the sky.

"Look at that!" Rachel pointed to a hot-air balloon floating in the sky above the festival. The balloon was covered with red and orange stripes, and a large basket hung down from it. The fierce wind sent leaves and bits of paper whirling around it, but the balloon itself seemed to hang in midair without moving. A bright spurt of flame shot from the burner to heat the air in the balloon and keep it floating.

"That's strange," said Kirsty. "It doesn't seem to be affected by the wind at all!"

"Yes," Rachel agreed. "How can it stay so still with the wind blowing all around it?"

"The goblin must be hiding in it!"

Abigail exclaimed. "Only the magic Breeze Feather could protect the balloon from the wind like that."

Kirsty's eyes widened. "So we've finally found the goblin," she said. "But he's way up in the sky!"

Up, Up, and Away!

"How are we going to get up there?"
Rachel asked.

"Easy!" Abigail told her. "We use fairy
magic!"

The girls immediately reached for
their shining golden lockets. The lockets
were full of magic fairy dust. They had
been special gifts from Titania, the
Fairy Queen. A pinch of the dust

would turn the girls into fairies, and
another pinch would turn them back into
humans again.

Rachel sprinkled
herself with sparkling
fairy dust, then laughed
with delight as she
shrank to fairy size. The
grass was as tall as she
was, and the buttercups
now seemed as big as
trees!

Kirsty did the
same, and turned
around to look at her
silvery wings. "Wow!
I'm a fairy again!"

"We have to hurry!"
Abigail said, zooming up into the air.

She was quickly followed by Kirsty and Rachel.

The higher Abigail and the girls flew, the more the wind tried to blow them off course. Kirsty and Rachel's wings soon felt really tired.

"Fly right behind me," Abigail urged the girls. "It might be easier for you."

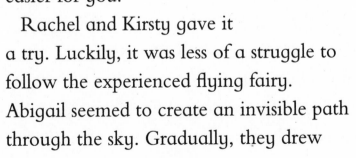

Rachel and Kirsty gave it a try. Luckily, it was less of a struggle to follow the experienced flying fairy. Abigail seemed to create an invisible path through the sky. Gradually, they drew

closer and closer to the balloon's
basket.

"We were right. Look!"
cried Kirsty.

An ugly face
peered over
the edge of the
balloon's basket. It
was a goblin with
pointed ears and a
big, lumpy nose.

"He's a very big
goblin," said Abigail
nervously.

"I don't think he's seen us yet,"
Rachel whispered. "Let's creep
up behind him."

The goblin was staring at Twiglet, who
was still barking down below. "Ha, ha!

Silly little doggy. You can't catch me!" he sneered. Kirsty and Rachel heard the goblin's tummy rumble. It sounded like mud being stirred in a bucket. The goblin gave a huge burp, and a blast of stinky breath blew over Rachel, Kirsty, and Abigail.

"Ugh!" Abigail held her nose.

"What a terrible smell!" complained Rachel. "What has that goblin been eating?"

"Can't catch me, doggy!" The goblin continued to taunt Twiglet, jumping up and down and waving a shining bronze feather.

Down on the ground, a strong gust of wind swept Twiglet off his feet. The puppy tumbled over, got up again, and shook his head angrily. Then he looked up and began barking even more loudly.

The goblin jumped
back, surprised. Then
he recovered. "I'm
safe up here!" he said
to himself, and
laughed.

Rachel was confused. *The goblin's afraid
of Twiglet,* she thought. *I wonder why.*

"He's holding the Breeze Feather!"
whispered Abigail. Her leaf-green eyes
flashed with anger.

"Yes. And he's using it to tease
poor Twiglet!" said Kirsty. "What a
mean goblin! We have to get that
feather back."

Rachel was thinking hard. "I've got a
plan," she told her friends. "Kirsty, you
land in the basket. Then Abigail can
make you human-size, and the two of

you can distract the goblin while I fly up and turn off the balloon's burner. The balloon will sink, and we'll have a better chance of getting the feather back once that goblin's back on the ground."

"That's a good idea," said Abigail. "But Kirsty and I will be very close to the goblin. Can you be quick, Rachel?"

"I will," Rachel promised.

"Okay, then here I go," Kirsty said. She checked to make sure that the goblin wasn't looking, and then flew up and over the edge of the basket. Abigail hovered next to her. With a wave of her wand, she turned Kirsty back to her normal size.

When he saw Kirsty, the goblin's eyes grew as big as golf balls. "Who are you?" he demanded.

"I'm Kirsty, a friend of the Weather Fairies," Kirsty declared firmly.

"And I'm Abigail the Breeze Fairy," Abigail added in her soft, musical voice.

The goblin glared at Abigail. "Boo!" he shouted, and lunged at her.

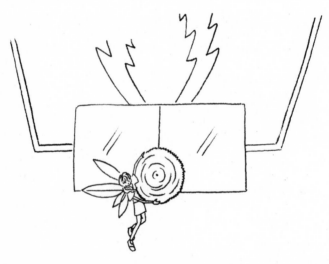

Abigail fluttered out of his reach, and the goblin snorted with laughter.

Just then, Kirsty saw Rachel overhead, turning off the burner. *So far so good,* she thought. *The goblin hasn't noticed Rachel.*

The goblin scowled at Kirsty. "Get off my balloon!" he roared.

"That's not very nice," Kirsty said calmly.

"I don't care!" snapped the goblin. He looked at Abigail slyly. "I know what you want and you're not going to get it!" he said, waving the Breeze Feather.

A huge gust of wind rocked the basket. Kirsty clung to the side as it tilted and wobbled.

The goblin snickered. "Too windy for you?"

"Your balloon's sinking," Kirsty answered.

"Don't be ridiculous!" sneered the goblin. Then he looked over the edge of the basket. "What?"

Down below, but getting closer all the time, Twiglet barked and growled.

The goblin's big nose twitched nervously.

Kirsty noticed a rip in the goblin's ragged clothing and remembered the piece of material in Twiglet's mouth. "Why are you afraid of the puppy?" she asked.

The goblin looked shifty. "I might have eaten his dinner," he replied sulkily.

No wonder his breath is so stinky! thought Kirsty.

"Now, tell me why this balloon's sinking!" demanded the goblin fiercely. "Or I'll wave the Breeze Feather and tip you out of the basket — like this!"

The basket rocked back and forth. Kirsty's heart pounded, but she hung on to the side. The goblin hardly moved, even though the basket shook and wobbled. He was perfectly balanced on his big, broad feet. He waved the Breeze Feather again, making the basket rock more than ever.

Kirsty reached nervously for her fairy locket. She would need her fairy wings if she was tipped out of the basket. But would she have time to use the fairy dust if she fell?

Flying High

"There's too much weight in this basket! That's why we're sinking," said Abigail.

The goblin glared at Kirsty. "You're too heavy. Get out!" he ordered.

Quick as a flash, Kirsty sprinkled herself with fairy dust from her locket and fluttered out of the goblin's way.

"We're still sinking!" the goblin cried.

Suddenly, his ugly face brightened. "But I don't need these heavy sandbags. They just help the balloon to land," he said. He grabbed the sandbags that hung around 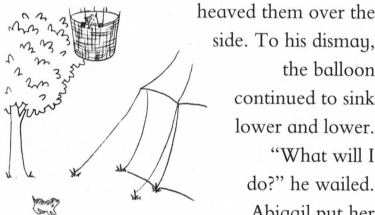 the edge of the basket and heaved them over the side. To his dismay, the balloon continued to sink lower and lower.

"What will I do?" he wailed.

Abigail put her hands on her hips. "You'll have to throw out that feather!" she told the goblin firmly.

"No!" snapped the goblin. "It's mine, and I'm keeping it! Besides, it's too light to make any difference."

Kirsty and Rachel hovered in the air behind Abigail. Would she be able to convince the goblin to get rid of the feather?

"It's a lot heavier than you think," Abigail said.

The goblin scowled. "What do you mean?"

"A pound of feathers weighs just the same as a pound of rocks, you know," Abigail replied.

Kirsty and Rachel laughed softly. *They* knew that a pound of anything weighs just the same as a pound of anything else! But goblins are foolish, and the girls guessed that Abigail was hoping to confuse this one.

127

The goblin blinked and scratched his head. Abigail's plan was working!

On the ground below, Twiglet barked and jumped up at the balloon. He seemed a lot closer now.

"Argh! Don't let it get me!" screamed the goblin. And in desperation, he flung the feather out of the basket. Abigail flew after it in a blur of golden wings, but the feather was caught by the wind and swept away.

"Come on!" shouted Rachel, flying after Abigail. Kirsty followed.

"The wind's too strong. I can't fly!" cried Rachel in panic.

The girls were tossed around by the wind. They flapped their wings and tried to regain control, but it was no use. They were drifting farther and farther from the Breeze Feather, and they couldn't even see Abigail through all the leaves and garbage swirling around them.

"We have to catch the Breeze Feather," shouted Kirsty. "Otherwise it could be lost forever!"

Bright and Breezy

Suddenly, Kirsty and Rachel caught a glimpse of Abigail flying to their rescue.

"Don't worry about us," Kirsty shouted above the wind.

"Just catch the Breeze Feather!" Rachel yelled.

Abigail must have heard them, because she nodded firmly and sped off after the feather again. She seemed about to grab it, when the wind snatched it away from her. Rachel let out a cry, but then she saw a rope of tiny golden leaves snake out from Abigail's wand and wrap around the Breeze Feather.

The tiny fairy pulled the feather toward her and finally managed to grab hold of it. She immediately waved it in a complicated pattern. "Wind, stop!" she ordered.

With a soft sigh, the roaring wind died. Kirsty and Rachel could immediately fly properly again.

Abigail flew over to join them. "It's wonderful to have the Breeze Feather back safe and sound!" she said happily.

"What about the goblin?" asked Kirsty.

Abigail frowned. "Leave him to me!" She pointed the feather at the hot-air balloon. "Wind, blow!" she commanded. An enormous puff of wind rocked the balloon.

The goblin hung over the basket. His face looked green. "I feel sick," he moaned.

"You shouldn't have eaten Twiglet's dinner, then!" Rachel told him.

"I wish I hadn't," replied the goblin gloomily. "It wasn't very good, anyway!"

Abigail waved the Breeze Feather a second time and the big red-and-orange balloon blew high into the sky. The goblin's cries faded as the balloon flew out of sight.

Kirsty, Rachel, and
Abigail flew to the
festival and slid
down one of the
tents to the ground.
Abigail waved her
wand, and Kirsty and
Rachel grew back to their
normal size. They peeked out
from behind the tent.

Now that the wind
had stopped,
people were
running around
organizing their
stalls. Over on
the lawn, Twiglet
was chewing
contentedly.

"Mr. McDougall gave Twiglet a dog biscuit to chew on," said Kirsty.

"I bet it tastes better than that goblin's clothes!" laughed Rachel.

"Kirsty!" called Kirsty's gran.

Abigail quickly zoomed onto Kirsty's shoulder and hid beneath her hair.

"Gran!" Suddenly, Kirsty remembered what had happened to her gran's cake. So why was her gran wearing such a big smile?

"I won first prize!" said Mrs. Tate, her eyes shining. "The judge said my cake was delicious. He couldn't help tasting it when it was all over his face!"

The girls were just congratulating Mrs. Tate when Mrs. Adelstrop stomped past, scowling.

Kirsty's gran chuckled. "She's won first prize for the last three years. It's time someone else had a chance!"

Rachel and Kirsty laughed. And only they heard the silvery giggling that came from under Kirsty's hair.

"Now I have to go," said Gran. "My best friend, Mable, is hoping to win a prize in one of the vegetable competitions!"

Kirsty and Rachel waved good-bye.

"We should go and give Doodle his magic feather back," said Kirsty.

The girls and Abigail headed home.

It was quiet and sunny now, and a warm summer breeze gently rustled through the leaves on Twisty Lane. "Everything's back to normal," said Rachel happily.

"For now," Kirsty added.

Back at Kirsty's house, Abigail flew straight up to the barn roof and carefully put the Breeze Feather into Doodle's tail.

The weather vane rooster shimmered in a magic haze of gold. And then he fizzed into life and shook himself. Fabulous copper sparkles flew into the air, making Rachel and Kirsty gasp. Doodle's fiery feathers were magnificent.

Doodle shifted to settle the Breeze Feather properly into place, where it glimmered and glowed. Then he looked straight at Rachel and Kirsty. "Jack —" he squawked, and opened his beak as if to speak again, but the color of his feathers faded. Doodle became a rusty old weather vane once more.

"He's trying to tell us something," said Kirsty.

"Last time, he said 'Beware,'" Rachel reminded Kirsty. "So now we have 'Beware Jack. . . .' I wonder what he wanted to say next?"

Abigail floated down from the roof. "I don't know," she said. "But keep your eyes open. Jack Frost is always up to no good."

"We will," Kirsty promised.

"Now I must fly back to Fairyland," Abigail said. "Thank you again, Rachel and Kirsty."

"Good-bye, Abigail!" Kirsty said, and Rachel waved.

Abigail's wings flashed, and with a swirl of tiny golden leaves, she was gone.

Rachel and Kirsty smiled at each other, enjoying their fairy secret.

"Five more magic feathers to find!" whispered Kirsty.

"I wonder which one we'll find next," Rachel said.

Pearl
the Cloud
Fairy

For Jean, with love and thanks for
the many pearls of wisdom!

Special thanks to
Narinder Dhami

Missing Fidget

"What's the weather like today, Kirsty?" asked Rachel Walker eagerly. She pushed back her bedspread. "Do you think there's magic in the air?"

Kirsty Tate was standing at the bedroom window, staring out over the garden. "It seems like a normal day."

She sighed, with a disappointed look on her face. "The sky's gray and cloudy."

"Never mind." Rachel jumped out of bed and went to join her friend. "Remember what Titania, the Fairy Queen, told us. Don't look too hard for magic —"

"Because the magic will find you!" Kirsty finished with a smile.

Rachel and Kirsty shared a very special secret. They were friends with fairies! When Jack Frost had put a spell on the seven Rainbow Fairies and banished them to Rainspell Island, Rachel and Kirsty helped them return to Fairyland. Now Jack Frost was up to no good again — this time with the Weather Fairies. And once again, the Fairy King and Queen had asked Rachel and Kirsty for help.

"Look at Doodle." Rachel pointed at the weather-vane rooster, which sat on top of the old barn. "Don't you think he looks a little happier, now that he has two of his tail feathers back?"

Kirsty nodded. "Let's hope we find all

of his feathers before you go home," she replied. "Then the weather in Fairyland can get back to normal again!"

Doodle the rooster had a very important job. With his seven magic tail feathers and the help of the Weather Fairies, Doodle controlled Fairyland's weather. But then Jack Frost sent his mean goblin servants to steal Doodle's feathers. Doodle chased the goblins into the human world — but without his magic, and away from Fairyland, he changed into an ordinary, rusty weather vane!

Kirsty's dad had found the weather vane lying in the park, and brought it home to put on the roof of the barn. He had no idea what a magical creature Doodle really was!

Now the weather in Fairyland was a
big mess — and it would be a mess until
Rachel and Kirsty got all of Doodle's
feathers back and sent him home.

"Well, we're off to a good start," said
Rachel. "With the help of Crystal the
Snow Fairy and Abigail the Breeze Fairy,
we've already found two feathers!"

The King and Queen had promised
Kirsty and Rachel that each of the
Weather Fairies would come to help
them find the feathers.

"Girls, are you awake?" Kirsty's mom called from downstairs. "Breakfast's ready."

"Coming!" Kirsty shouted back.

"I wish we knew what Doodle was trying to tell us yesterday," said Rachel,  as she and Kirsty ran downstairs. Each time one of Doodle's tail feathers had been replaced, the rooster had come to life. The first time, he squawked "Beware!" The second time, he managed to say the word "Jack," before turning to metal again.

"I'm sure it was something about Jack Frost," Kirsty said thoughtfully. "But what?"

"Maybe he'll tell us if we find another feather!" Rachel suggested. The girls went into the kitchen. Mr. Tate was setting the table, and Kirsty's mom was making toast.

"Morning, you two," said Mr. Tate with a smile, as the girls sat down. "What are you planning to do today?"

Before Kirsty or Rachel could answer
him, there was a knock at the back door.

"I wonder who that
could be!" Mrs. Tate
said, raising her
eyebrows. "It's still
pretty early."

"I'll get it," said
Kirsty, who was
closest.

She opened the
door. There were
Mr. and Mrs.
Twitching, the Tates' neighbors.

"Oh, Kirsty, good morning," said Mr. Twitching. "We're sorry to bother you, but we were hoping you might have seen Fidget?"

Kirsty frowned, trying to remember. She knew Fidget, the Twitchings' fluffy tabby cat, very well, but she hadn't seen her for the last day or two. "I haven't seen her lately," she replied.

"Oh, dear," Mrs. Twitching said, looking upset. "She didn't come home for her dinner last night."

"Come in and ask Mom and Dad," Kirsty suggested,

opening the door wider. "Maybe they've seen her."

As Mr. and Mrs. Twitching walked into the kitchen, Kirsty blinked. For a minute, she thought she'd seen strange wisps of pale smoke curling and drifting over the neighbors' heads.

Jack Frost

Rachel & Kirsty

Goldie the Sunshine Fairy

Crystal the Snow Fairy

King Oberon & Queen Titania

RAINBOW magic™
THE WEATHER FAIRIES

Abigail the Breeze Fairy

She glanced at Rachel and her parents, but they didn't seem to have noticed anything unusual. Kirsty shook her head. Maybe she was just imagining it. . . .

Magic in the Air

"When was the last time you saw Fidget?" asked Kirsty's mom as she poured some coffee for the Twitchings.

"Yesterday afternoon," Mrs. Twitching replied. "It's very strange, because usually she doesn't miss a single meal."

"Kirsty and I could help you look for her," suggested Rachel.

"Good idea," Kirsty agreed, finishing her cereal. "Let's go now."

"And I'll check our garden and the barn," added Mr. Tate.

As Kirsty and Rachel got up from the table, Kirsty stared extra-hard at the Twitchings' heads. She thought she could see wisps of smoke there again, but they were so pale and misty, it was hard to be sure.

"Rachel," Kirsty said quietly as they headed outside, "did you notice anything funny about the Twitchings today?"

Rachel looked confused. "What do you mean?"

Kirsty told her about the wisps of smoke. "I'm not sure if I really saw them or not," she finished.

"Do you think they could have been magic?" Rachel asked.

Kirsty felt a thrill of excitement. "Maybe," she said eagerly. "While we're looking for Fidget, we'd better keep our eyes open for magic, too!"

The girls walked into the village, keeping their eyes peeled for the tabby cat, but there was no sign of her.

"I hope Fidget isn't lost for good," Kirsty said, looking around. "Oh!"

Kirsty hadn't been watching where she was going, and she'd bumped into someone. "I'm so sorry," Kirsty said politely.

The woman glared at her. "Why don't you be more careful?" she said grumpily, and hurried off.

"Well!" Rachel gasped. "That wasn't very nice."

But Kirsty looked confused. "That was Mrs. Hill, one of my mom's friends, and she's usually *very* nice," she said. "I wonder what's wrong?"

Rachel nudged her. "Look over there," she whispered.

Outside the post office, two men were arguing. They both looked very grouchy. Then Mrs. Burke, who ran the post office, came out to see what was going on. Kirsty was surprised to see that her usually happy face was grumpy and sad.

"There's something strange happening," she whispered to Rachel as they went into the park. "Everybody's in a terrible mood. Look at the kids on the swings."

Rachel stared at the children in the playground. They didn't seem to be having fun at all. Every single one of them looked sad! They didn't even cheer up when the ice-cream truck stopped close by.

The girls stopped at the park gate.

"I think we've been all over

Wetherbury, and there's no sign of Fidget anywhere." Kirsty sighed, glancing at her watch. "We'd better go home, Rachel. It's almost time for lunch."

Rachel nodded. "We can always keep searching later this afternoon."

The girls turned back toward the Tates' house. On the way, they passed the tiny movie theater. The Saturday morning show had just finished, and the audience was pouring out. Just like everyone else, the people looked grouchy.

"It must have been a sad movie," Rachel whispered to Kirsty.

"But it wasn't," Kirsty replied, frowning. "Look." She pointed to the poster outside the movie theater.

"This hilarious film is a must. You'll split your sides laughing," Rachel read. "Well, the audience definitely didn't find it very funny," she continued. "Look at their faces." Kirsty stared at the people walking gloomily out of the theater. Suddenly, her heart began to pound. There they were again! She could definitely see cloudy smoke drifting over people's heads, just like she'd noticed

over her next-door neighbors. "Look, Rachel!" She nudged her friend. "There's that smoke again."

Rachel squinted at the people who were all frowning. For a minute, she thought Kirsty was seeing things. But then she spotted them, too — thin, wispy trails of smoke, hovering over the heads of the people like little clouds.

"It must be fairy magic!" Rachel said excitedly. "I'll bet those aren't wisps of smoke at all. They're magic clouds!"

"Maybe," Kirsty agreed, her eyes lighting up. "We could be close to finding another magic feather!"

The girls rushed home. When they entered the house, the first

thing they noticed were the clouds hovering over Mr. and Mrs. Tate!

"Did you find Fidget?" asked Kirsty's mom. She was sitting on the couch, reading a book. The little white cloud over her head was tinted with pink, like a cloud in a sunset.

"No," Kirsty replied, staring at the gray cloud over her dad.

"Oh, dear," Mr. Tate said, looking sad.

"I think the goblin with the magic Cloud Feather must be close by," Rachel whispered to Kirsty as they ate their sandwiches.

Kirsty nodded. "After lunch, let's go up to my bedroom and plan our next move," she said. "These clouds are beginning to worry me."

"Me, too," Rachel agreed.

As soon as they'd finished their food, the girls ran upstairs. Kirsty threw open her bedroom door.

"Hello!" called a tiny voice. "I thought you would never come!"

There, sitting on the windowsill and swinging her legs below her, was Pearl the Cloud Fairy.

Goblin Hunting

Pearl was resting her chin on her hands, and she also looked gloomy. She wore a beautiful pink and white dress with a full skirt, and in her hand, she held a pretty pink wand. The wand had a fluffy white tip. Little pink and white sunset clouds drifted and swirled out of it.

To Kirsty's amazement, a tiny gray cloud hovered over Pearl's head. "Oh, Pearl! You have a rain cloud, too!" Kirsty said.

"I know." Pearl sighed, then her eyes flashed with annoyance. "It's because one of those nasty goblins is using the magic Cloud Feather — and he's doing it all wrong!" she snapped.

"We think the goblin must be very close, because everyone in Wetherbury

seems to have a cloud over them,"
Rachel told Pearl.

"I'm sure you're right," Pearl said.
"This is definitely fairy magic, so
that mean old goblin can't be far
away!" She fluttered up into the
air, leaving a trail of shining
pink and white clouds
behind her. "Even you
two are beginning to
get clouds now!"
she added.

The girls rushed
over to the mirror
to look. Sure
enough, tiny gray
clouds were starting to
form over their heads.

"Should we go find the Cloud Feather?" Kirsty asked eagerly.

Pearl and Rachel both cheered up at that suggestion. Pearl zoomed over to hide herself in Rachel's jacket pocket. Then they all headed out into the village.

This time, Rachel and Kirsty could see the clouds over people's heads much more clearly. Some were a pretty pink or orange color, and the people underneath them seemed quiet and dreamy.

174

Other clouds were black and stormy, and the people under those looked gloomy and annoyed. Some clouds were drizzling tiny raindrops, making their people look very sad. And a few very angry people had clouds with little lightning bolts over their heads.

"Look." Rachel nudged Kirsty as a man with a lightning cloud hurried past, scowling.

"His hair's standing straight up like he got an electric shock!"

"Pearl," Kirsty whispered. "Why hasn't anyone else noticed the clouds?"

Pearl popped her head out of Rachel's pocket. "Only magic beings like fairies can see them," she replied. "And you two, because you're helping us."

"The clouds are getting bigger," said Rachel, staring at a woman who passed by with an enormous rain cloud over her head.

"We must be getting closer to the feather!" Pearl said eagerly.

"But where can it be?" Kirsty wondered. "We're almost out of the village now." She stopped and looked around. Suddenly, she gasped, and pointed at a building to their left. "Look at the candy factory!"

The candy factory stood right on the edge of Wetherbury. A stream of small pink and white clouds were puffing out of the tall brick chimney.

"The goblin must be hiding inside the factory," Pearl cried, whizzing out of Rachel's pocket and fluttering up into the air. "It's time to rescue the Cloud Feather!"

A Sticky Situation

"Come on," Rachel said. "Let's go inside."

The girls and Pearl rushed over to the door. But their hearts sank when they saw the big, heavy padlock.

"Of course, it's Saturday. The factory's closed." Kirsty said, looking disappointed. "What are we going to do?"

They stood and thought for a minute. Then Rachel glanced up, and a smile spread across her face. "Look!" she said, pointing. "There's an air vent near the roof. We have our magic fairy dust. Let's turn ourselves into fairies. Then we can all fly in through the air vent."

The Fairy Queen had given Kirsty and Rachel gold lockets full of fairy dust, which they could use to turn themselves into fairies whenever they needed to.

"Good idea!" Pearl laughed, clapping her hands happily.

Quickly, Rachel and
Kirsty opened their
lockets and sprinkled
some fairy dust over
themselves. Almost
immediately, they
began to shrink, and
beautiful shimmering
fairy wings grew from
their backs.

"Come on," Pearl cried, zooming
back and forth impatiently. "Up we go!"
And she flew up to the air vent in the
wall.

Kirsty and Rachel flew after her. Pearl
slipped through the vent first, and the
two girls followed. They all stopped
inside and gazed around the factory.

"Wow!" Kirsty gasped, her eyes wide.

Lots of big silver machines were busy making all kinds of different candy. Peppermints poured out of one machine, while long strings of strawberry licorice came out of another. Soft ice cream fizzed into paper cups, and pink and white marshmallows bounced along a moving conveyor belt. Chocolate bars

were being wrapped in gold foil, while a
different machine wrapped caramel
candies in shiny silver paper. There were
large sticky lollipops and striped candy
canes in every color and flavor.

"Isn't this amazing?" asked Rachel.
"Look at all the different kinds of
candy!"

Kirsty looked confused. "But the people who work here wouldn't have left all the machines on, would they?" she pointed out.

Pearl grinned. "I bet they turned them off, but somebody else has turned them on again."

"The goblin!" Kirsty exclaimed. "Where is he?"

"Let's split up and see if we can find him," Pearl replied.

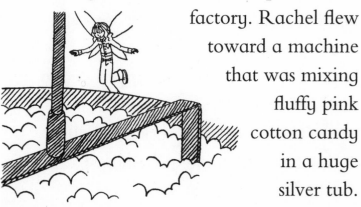

They flew off to different parts of the factory. Rachel flew toward a machine that was mixing fluffy pink cotton candy in a huge silver tub.

She looked at the machine for a minute and was about to fly on, but then she heard the sound of someone loudly smacking his lips.

Rachel flew down to take a closer look. There, lying with his back to her, on a huge, fluffy pink cloud, was the goblin! He was greedily scooping up sticky handfuls of cotton candy and munching them happily. He was quite chubby — probably from stuffing himself with so much cotton candy, Rachel thought.

She flew a little closer and peeked over the goblin's shoulder to see if she could spot the magic Cloud Feather. There it was, in his hand! Tiny pink and white clouds drifted from it as the goblin waved it in the air.

I have to tell Kirsty and Pearl, Rachel thought. She turned to fly away, but as she did, one wing brushed the goblin's shoulder. With a yelp of surprise, the goblin reached up and grabbed Rachel with one hand.

"You're not getting my feather!" he shouted, and stuffed Rachel inside one of the pink clouds that was drifting by.

Poor Rachel was trapped! She tried to push her way out of the cloud, but she couldn't make a hole in it. The cloud drifted farther and farther away from the goblin.

"Kirsty! Pearl!" Rachel called as loudly as she could. "HELP!"

Kirsty heard her friend's voice right away. She turned and saw the cloud with Rachel inside. It was floating past the marshmallow machine.

To Kirsty's horror, the cloud was heading straight toward the factory's tall chimney.

"Oh no!" Kirsty gasped. "If that cloud floats up the chimney, we'll never get Rachel back!"

Cotton Candy Clouds

Quickly, Pearl flew over to Kirsty.
"Which cloud is Rachel in?" she asked.

"That one . . ." Kirsty began, pointing.
Then she stopped. There were so many
clouds floating around, she'd lost sight of
Rachel. "Oh, I don't know anymore,
Pearl. That awful goblin did it!" she said.

"I have a few things to say to him! Can you make me human-size again?"

Pearl nodded. "Don't worry," she said, "I'll find Rachel. I promise. You get the feather back."

With a wave of her wand, Pearl turned Kirsty back to her normal size. Then she flew off to search through the clouds. Kirsty stormed over to the goblin. She was usually scared of the nasty creatures — especially since Jack Frost had used his magic to make them even bigger than before. But Kirsty was so annoyed, she didn't care. Rachel was in danger, and it was all the goblin's fault.

The goblin was lying on top of his fluffy cloud, still eating cotton candy. When he saw Kirsty marching toward him, he looked nervous. Quickly, he stuffed the Cloud Feather right into his mouth.

"Give me that feather!" Kirsty demanded.

"Wha' fe'er?" the goblin spluttered, trying to keep his mouth closed.

Kirsty frowned. How was she going to get the feather out of the goblin's mouth? Just then, she spotted a peppermint stick

lying on the floor. That gave her an
idea. She picked it up, and began tickling
the bottom of the goblin's leathery foot!

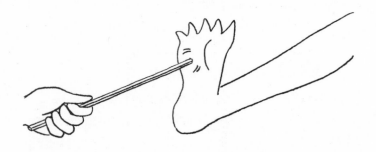

The goblin began to laugh, but he kept
his mouth shut. "Shtop it," he mumbled.
But then he couldn't hold his laughter in
anymore. "Oh, ha ha ha," he laughed.
As his laughter burst out, so did the
magic Cloud Feather!

Kirsty tried to grab the feather, but the

goblin was quicker.

"Oh no!" He grinned,
snatching the feather
away. "This is *my*
feather! I'm the only
one who knows how
to make it work."

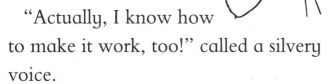

"Actually, I know how
to make it work, too!" called a silvery
voice.

Kirsty turned to see Pearl flying toward
them. To Kirsty's relief, she was pulling a
pink cloud behind her with Rachel
inside.

Rachel's head was sticking out of a hole in the cloud, and she grinned at Kirsty. "Hey, this cloud's made of cotton candy!" she called. "And it's delicious. I can eat my way out!". She took another big bite of the cloud.

Pearl flew down to Kirsty and the goblin. "I can make the clouds do all sorts of things," she said. "They will float exactly where I tell them to. I can even make them dance around me." She held out her hand to the goblin. "Why don't you give me the feather and let me show you?"

The goblin looked sly. "No, it's mine!" he said. "Anyway, I can do those tricks myself."

"Go on, then," Pearl challenged.

The goblin began to concentrate. He waved the feather around in the air. Very slowly, all the clouds in the room drifted toward him. He twirled the feather, and the clouds began to spin around him in a circle, faster and faster. "See?" the goblin bragged.

"OK, you know what to do, Rachel," Pearl whispered to her.

Pearl let go of Rachel's cotton candy cloud, and she and Kirsty watched as it flew over to the goblin. Rachel's cloud began to whirl around him with the others. It got closer and closer to the goblin. Then, suddenly, as her cloud sped past the goblin's hand, Rachel stuck her arm out and grabbed the Cloud Feather!

A Silver Lining

"Give that back!" the goblin shouted.
Every time Rachel's cloud flew past him,
he tried to grab back the feather, but he
missed over and over again.

The clouds were spinning around so
fast now that Rachel was getting very
dizzy. "Help!" she called. "Somebody
stop this cloud!"

Pearl swooped down and plucked the feather out of Rachel's hand. Then she waved it in a special pattern, and the clouds began to slow down and drift away.

Kirsty caught Rachel's cloud with one hand, and she pulled it open to free her friend.

Rachel dizzily tumbled out. The goblin was dizzy, too, from watching all the clouds spinning around his head.

He was walking in circles, looking for the Cloud Feather. When he saw that Pearl had it, he lunged forward and grabbed for her. Pearl flew out of the way just in time, but the goblin lost his balance. He tripped and fell headfirst into the candy wrapping machine!

The girls and Pearl watched in amazement as the yelling goblin was wrapped in a huge sheet of shiny silver paper. Then the goblin-shaped candy moved along the conveyor belt, and was wrapped with a sparkly silver ribbon.

"That serves him right!" Rachel laughed.

"Come on," said Pearl, smiling. "Let's get out of here before he unwraps himself!"

Kirsty sprinkled herself with fairy dust and immediately turned into a fairy again. Then the three friends flew out of the factory through the air vent. Outside, Pearl waved her magic wand and returned the girls to their normal size.

"I'd better make sure everyone else in Wetherbury gets back to normal right away!" Pearl laughed.

She waved her feather through the air in a complicated pattern. "That should do it," she said cheerfully. They set off for the Tates' house, and Pearl hid in Rachel's pocket again.

"Look," whispered Rachel, as they made their way through the village. "There aren't any clouds over people's heads anymore!"

"And everyone's happy and laughing again," added Kirsty. The kids playing in the park were all smiling now, and as the girls passed the post office, Mrs. Burke gave them a cheerful wave.

"I'll give Doodle his beautiful Cloud Feather back," Pearl said, when they arrived at the Tates' house. "He'll be so happy to see it!"

Rachel and Kirsty stood in the garden. They watched as Pearl flew up to the top of the barn. The fairy placed the Cloud Feather in Doodle's tail. A minute later, the rooster's feathers began to sparkle with fairy magic.

"Doodle's coming to life again!" Kirsty cried. "Listen up, Rachel!"

Doodle's feathers shimmered in the sun. "Frost w —!" he squawked. But the next minute, he was cold, hard metal again.

"Beware, Jack Frost w —" Kirsty said thoughtfully, as Pearl flew down to join them. "What does it mean?"

"I don't know," replied Pearl. "But be careful. Jack Frost won't want to lose any more magic feathers! And now I have to return to Fairyland."

The pretty fairy hugged Rachel and Kirsty, scattering little, shiny pink and white clouds around them. Then she fluttered up into the sky. "Good-bye!" she called, "And thank you! Good luck finding the other four weather feathers!"

"Good-bye!" called Kirsty and Rachel, waving.

Smiling, Pearl waved her wand at them and disappeared into the clouds.

The girls went into the house, where Mr. and Mrs. Tate were in the living room watching TV.

"Oh, Kirsty, Rachel, there you are," said Mrs. Tate, jumping to her feet. "The Twitchings called a little while ago and invited us over for coffee."

"And they said they have some good news for us," Mr. Tate added.

Kirsty and Rachel looked at each other.

"They must have found Fidget!" Kirsty exclaimed happily.

The girls hurried next door with Mr. and Mrs. Tate.

Mr. Twitching opened the door with a big smile on his face. "Come in," he said. "We've got a surprise for you!"

He led them into the living room, where Mrs. Twitching was kneeling on the rug next to a cat basket. A big, fluffy tabby cat was curled up inside.

"She's been a very busy girl," Mrs. Twitching said proudly. "Look!"

There in the basket were three tiny kittens, snuggled up close to their mom.

Two were tabby cats like Fidget, and one was black with a little white spot on the top of its head. They were so young, their eyes weren't even open yet.

"Oh, Rachel, aren't they beautiful?" Kirsty whispered, gently stroking the black and white kitten on its tiny head.

"We'll be looking for good homes for them when they're bigger," said Mr. Twitching. "But they can't leave their mom for eight or nine weeks."

"Oh!" Kirsty gasped, her eyes shining. "Maybe I could have one?"

"I don't see why not," Mrs. Tate said, smiling.

"Which one would you like, Kirsty?" Mrs. Twitching asked.

"This one," Kirsty said, stroking the black and white kitten again. It yawned sleepily.

"And I know the perfect name for her," Rachel said, smiling at her friend. "You can call her Pearl!"

Goldie
the Sunshine
Fairy

Dedicated to Liss Brothwell,
who is a little ray of sunshine

Special thanks to
Sue Mongredien

A Sunny Spell

"I feel like I'm going to melt," said Rachel Walker happily.

It was a hot summer afternoon and she and her friend, Kirsty Tate, were enjoying the sunshine in Kirsty's backyard. A bumblebee buzzed lazily around Mrs. Tate's sunflowers, and a single gust of wind blew through the yellow rosebushes.

The weather was so warm and sunny
that Mr. and Mrs. Tate had given the
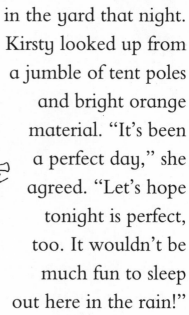 girls permission to camp out
in the yard that night.
Kirsty looked up from
a jumble of tent poles
and bright orange
material. "It's been
a perfect day," she
agreed. "Let's hope
tonight is perfect,
too. It wouldn't be
much fun to sleep
out here in the rain!"
Rachel laughed, and then started
untangling tent poles with her friend.
"I think I'd rather take a shower in the
morning, not in the middle of the night,"
she agreed.

Kirsty held up some poles. "Right. So how do we put this thing together?" she asked brightly.

Rachel scratched her head. "Well . . ." she began.

"Need some help?" came a voice from behind them.

"Dad!" said Kirsty, relieved. "Yes, please. We —" She turned to look at her father and burst out laughing.

Rachel spun around to see what was so funny. She had to bite her lip not to laugh, too. Mr. Tate was wearing the most enormous sunglasses she had ever seen!

Mr. Tate looked very pleased with himself. He wiggled the glasses up and down on his nose. "Do you like my new shades?" he asked.

"Well, yes," Kirsty said, trying to keep a straight face. "They're very . . . summery."

Mr. Tate knelt down and started putting the tent together. "The weather has been so strange all week, I didn't know whether to buy the sunglasses or not," he said. "I just hope it doesn't start snowing again!"

Rachel and Kirsty looked at each other but didn't say anything. The two friends shared a very special secret. They knew *exactly* why the weather had been so strange — Jack Frost had been messing it all up.

Doodle, the weather vane rooster, usually controlled the weather in Fairyland with his seven magic tail feathers and the help of the Weather Fairies. But mean Jack Frost had sent his goblins to steal Doodle's feathers. Without the feathers, the weather in Fairyland and the real world had gone completely crazy. Rachel and Kirsty were helping the Weather Fairies to get them back, but until then, Doodle was just a regular weather vane on top of the Tates' barn.

221

The day before, with the help of Pearl the Cloud Fairy, Kirsty and Rachel had returned the Cloud Feather to Doodle. But even though the girls had found the Snow Feather, the Breeze Feather, and the Cloud Feather, they still had four feathers left to find.

"There!" said Mr. Tate, stepping back and admiring the finished tent. "It's all yours."

"Thanks, Dad," Kirsty said as he walked away. She put two sleeping bags inside the tent and then flopped down on the grass. "Phew!" she said, and whistled. "It's still so hot! I hope it cools down soon, or we'll never be able to sleep in

there." Rachel was frowning and looking
at her watch.

"Kirsty," she said slowly. "Have
you noticed where the sun is?"

Kirsty looked up and
pointed. "Right there,
in the sky," she
replied.

"Yes, but look
how high it is,"
Rachel insisted.
"It hasn't even
started setting yet."

Kirsty glanced
at her watch. "But
it's seven-thirty,"
she said, frowning.
"That can't be
right."

Rachel and Kirsty grinned at each other proudly.

"The goblin who has the Sunshine Feather can't be far away," Goldie continued, looking up at the sky. The sun still blazed as brightly as ever.

"That's what we thought, too," Kirsty said. "There's a farm on the other side of this field. Should we start looking there?"

"Good idea," Goldie replied cheerfully. Her face fell as soon as she turned back toward the cornfield. Popcorn was still whizzing through the air like hot white bumblebees. "But is there another way across the field?"

Goblin on the Loose!

"I don't like the idea of dodging that popcorn again." Goldie sighed. She leaned back to examine a little mark on one of her wings. "I almost burned myself last time."

"There's a path that runs down the side of the field to the farm," Kirsty told her. "I'll ask Mom if we can go for a quick walk before bedtime."

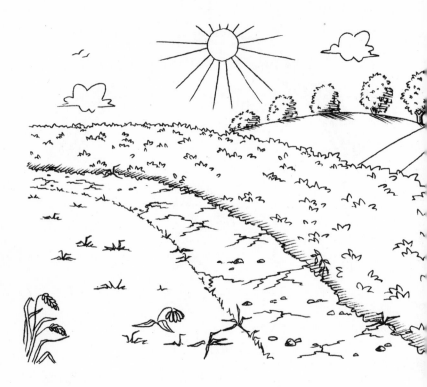

Minutes later, the three of them were on
their way. The air was shimmering with
heat. There were cracks in the ground
where the dirt had become hardened by
the sun, flowers wilted along the sides
of the path, and the grass had turned dry

and brown. There wasn't the slightest breath of wind in the air. Once the girls and Goldie reached the farm, they started searching for the goblin.

First, they peeked into the stables. Two very hot horses were inside, hiding from the sun. "Hello," Goldie said. "You haven't seen a goblin hanging around here, have you?"

One of the horses shook her mane.

"All we've seen today is this stable," she said. "And there are no goblins in here."

"It's too hot to go outside," the other horse whinnied.

Next, the girls and Goldie slipped into the barn where the cows stayed. The cows were all half-asleep in the heat. There was no goblin there, either!

At last, the three friends came to the duck pond. They wondered if the goblin might be cooling off in the water, but there was no sign of him — or the Sunshine Feather.

"You should ask the pigs," one duck quacked helpfully from a shady spot in the cattails. "They've been grumbling

all day about something. Plus, pigs are nosy. They're always sniffing around! If there's a goblin on the farm, they'll know about it."

Goldie politely thanked the duck.

"I think I hear the pigs over this way," Rachel said, walking around the side of the farmhouse. Soon they could all hear the pigs grunting and squealing. The duck was right! The pigs seemed very upset about something. But they all turned to look curiously at Goldie when she flew over to them.

Goldie fluttered down and
landed on the biggest
pig's snout. "What's
wrong?" she asked
kindly.

The pig squinted at
the golden fairy in front
of his little blue eyes. "It's
like this," he began in a
squeaky voice. "It's been so hot that
the farmer added some cold water
to the mudhole, so that us pigs could
keep nice and cool." He twitched his
ears indignantly. "But someone else has
stolen our spot in the mud — and he
won't let us in!"

"It's not fair," a piglet squealed,
running up to Rachel and Kirsty. "We're
so hot! It's not fair!"

"No, it's not," Kirsty agreed, giving
him a pat on the head.

"That sounds like the kind of trick a
goblin would play!" Rachel pointed out.
"Where is the mudhole?"

The pigs gave them directions, and the
girls set off for the mudhole with Goldie
flying above them. It seemed to get
hotter and hotter as they walked. Rachel
crossed her fingers. She was sure that
they would find a goblin in the mud.

Who else would be mean enough to stop the pigs from cooling off in their own mud pool?

The girls hadn't been walking for very long when they heard someone singing in a croaky voice:

"I've been having so much fun
Blasting out this golden sun.
It's roasting, toasting, popcorn weather.
Oh, how I love my Sunshine Feather!"

Kirsty, Rachel, and Goldie all ducked
behind a nearby tree and carefully
peeked out. There, covered in thick, wet
mud, was an extremely cheerful goblin.
He waved the Sunshine Feather in the air
while he sang. Each time the feather
moved, golden sunbeams flooded from its
tip, making the air feel even hotter.

Every time he got to the end of his
song, the goblin started all over again,
splashing his feet in the mud as he sang.
"I've been having so much fun . . ."

"What should we do?" Kirsty
whispered. The
goblin held on
to the feather
so tightly, it
looked like
it would be
impossible to take
it away from him.

Goldie twirled
around in frustration.

"I hate seeing him with my Sunshine
Feather," she muttered, folding her arms
across her chest. "Look, he got mud all
over it!"

Rachel frowned. "Maybe we could distract him somehow, then run over and grab the feather while he's looking the other way."

"I don't know about running through all that slippery mud," Kirsty said quietly, eyeing the mudhole doubtfully. "We'll probably fall over. And look, the goblin is right in the middle of it. He'll be able to see us coming way before we get there."

They moved farther away from the mudhole so that they could figure out what to do next without the goblin overhearing. But after a few minutes, Rachel held up her hand. "Shh! What's that noise?" she whispered in alarm.

A Confused Goblin

Kirsty, Rachel, and Goldie held their breath and listened to the strange new sound. It was a loud, wheezing, rumbling noise, somewhere between a grunt and a hiss.

Grumble-sshhh, grumble-sshhh, grumble-sshhh . . .

The sound was coming from the direction

of the mudhole. Kirsty and Rachel crept back to the tree and peeked out from behind it, wondering what sort of terrifying creature had appeared.

When Rachel saw what was making the noise, though, she had to clap her hand over her mouth to stop herself from laughing out loud. The wheezy rumble was coming from the goblin — he was snoring!

"At least he isn't singing anymore," Kirsty whispered, laughing.

Goldie fluttered her wings
hopefully when she saw
that the goblin was
asleep, and she flew
a little closer to the
Sunshine Feather. But
her face fell when she
saw just how tightly the
goblin was clutching
the feather to his chest.
Goldie flew back to the girls,
shaking her head. "If I try to pull it out
of his hand, the goblin is sure to wake
up," she told them. "How are we going
to get that feather?"

Kirsty smiled. "Maybe we could . . ."
she began thoughtfully. Then she grinned
from ear to ear. "Yes! That could work!"
she said.

Without another word, Kirsty began running back toward her house. "I'll be back in a minute," she called over her shoulder.

Rachel and Goldie watched her go. They were both dying to know what Kirsty was up to. Luckily, they didn't have to wait very long. When Kirsty came back, she looked quite different!

"What is she wearing?" Goldie whispered to Rachel as Kirsty ran toward them.

"Her dad's sunglasses," Rachel replied, staring at her friend in disbelief. She was starting to wonder if Kirsty had been in the sun for too long. Why had she brought the enormous sunglasses back with her? And why was she carrying a fishing pole?

Kirsty grinned at the confused expressions on her friends' faces. "I'll explain everything," she promised, propping the fishing pole and sunglasses up in the tree branches. "But first, Rachel and I need to shrink to fairy size."

Both Kirsty and Rachel had been given beautiful gold lockets by the Fairy Queen. Inside each locket was magical fairy dust. A tiny pinch of the sparkling dust turned the girls into fairies in the blink of an eye!

Kirsty and Rachel both pulled out their lockets and sprinkled themselves with fairy dust. It glittered a bright sunshine-yellow in the light and then — *whoosh* — they shrank smaller and smaller and smaller. The tree next to them looked enormous as the girls shrank to Goldie's size.

Kirsty and Rachel fluttered their wings happily. They both loved being fairies!

"Now," Kirsty said. "Let's fly up into the tree and I'll tell you my plan."

The three friends all perched near the fishing pole, and Goldie and Rachel watched as Kirsty carefully balanced the sunglasses on the end of the fishhook.

"We're going to let the fishing line out
very slowly," Kirsty said, "and lower
the sunglasses right
down onto the
goblin's nose."

"Why?" Rachel
asked, confused.

"I don't know
if they'll look
good on him,"
Goldie said.

Kirsty shook
her head, trying
not to laugh.

"With sunglasses
on, everything will look
dark to him," she whispered.
"With a bit of luck, the goblin will
think the Sunshine Feather is broken!"

Goldie clapped her hands in delight. "Oh, what a great idea!" she cried. "I love to play tricks on those mean old goblins."

Very carefully, Kirsty, Rachel, and Goldie turned the handle of the fishing rod and lowered the sunglasses all the way down in front of the goblin. Kirsty held her breath as the sunglasses landed right on his big nose. Perfect! The girls reeled in the fishing line, and Goldie waved her wand in the air. It released a stream of magical fairy dust. Little golden sparkles fizzed and popped like firecrackers around the goblin's head until he woke up with a start.

He opened his eyes and blinked when he saw that everything around him had gotten dark. "My feather's broken!" he moaned, giving it a shake. "Shine, sun!" he commanded.

Of course, the girls knew that the Sunshine Feather wasn't broken. As soon as the goblin shook it, the sun became brighter than ever. But as far as the goblin could see, the world was still dark.

He waved the feather again. "I said, shine!" he ordered. The sun shone like it was the middle of the day, but Goldie and her friends realized that the goblin thought it looked like night. He shook the feather two more times and the sun shone

hotter and brighter, but the goblin saw only darkness. As far as he could tell, the Sunshine Feather was not working. "Broken!" he announced angrily, and he threw the feather away in disgust.

Just then, Goldie darted out of the tree like a little golden firework. While the goblin was still muttering to himself, Goldie swooped down and grabbed the feather from the mud.

"Thank you!" she called, hugging the feather tightly as she flew back to the girls. Kirsty's plan had worked!

With another sprinkle of fairy dust, Rachel and Kirsty turned themselves human again. They grabbed the fishing rod and started scrambling down from the tree.

But the goblin spotted the girls and jumped to his feet. As he did, the sunglasses bounced on his nose.

"Sunglasses?" he exclaimed, reaching up to grab the glasses in confusion. He pushed them onto the top of his head and squinted at the girls in the dazzling sunlight. "You tricked me!" he yelled when he saw Goldie clutching the Sunshine Feather. "Come back with that feather!"

Kirsty and Rachel looked at each other
in fear. Now that Jack Frost's goblins
were so big, they seemed scarier than
ever. And this one looked *very* angry at
having been tricked.

He shook his fist and headed straight
toward the girls.

"*Run!*" shouted Kirsty.

Happy Pigs

Rachel grabbed Kirsty's hand and they both sprinted toward the farmhouse as fast as their feet would carry them. The goblin wasn't far behind, making a horrible growling sound in his throat as he ran.

"Give me back that feather! Give it back!" he yelled angrily.

Rachel's heart thumped in her chest. The goblin was closing in on them. She could hear his breathing. The goblin stretched out his hand to grab her and Rachel gasped.

"Got y —" the goblin began. Then his voice turned from anger to confusion. "Hey! What's going on?"

In a swirl of dancing sunbeams, Goldie
had waved the Sunshine Feather and
pointed it straight at the goblin. Now
the sun beat down fiercely upon him —
and the thick mud that covered
him started to dry rapidly. As his legs
became stiff and heavy with the
hardening mud, the goblin slowed down.
Then the mud dried completely, and the
goblin couldn't move at all.

"No-o-o!" he wailed.

Despite having been so scared just a
few seconds before, the girls found
themselves smiling at the goblin now.
"It's a goblin statue!" Rachel exclaimed,
laughing.

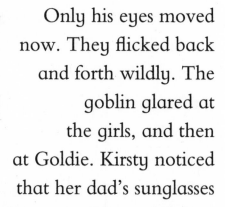

Only his eyes moved
now. They flicked back
and forth wildly. The
goblin glared at
the girls, and then
at Goldie. Kirsty noticed
that her dad's sunglasses
were still perched on top of the goblin's
head. She took a cautious step toward
him, then another. The goblin didn't
move, so Kirsty marched right up
to him and carefully grabbed
the glasses.

"I'll take these back now, I think," she said. "If I'd known that these sunglasses would be so useful, I'd never have laughed at Dad for wearing them!" she told Rachel.

Goldie and the girls made their way back to the farmhouse. The pigs were waiting expectantly for them.

"The mudhole is all yours again," Goldie told the pigs in her sweet voice. "You'll see a new goblin statue nearby," she added. "But don't worry. I don't think he'll be in any hurry to go back into the mud."

The pigs grunted happily and trotted off toward their cool mud pool. The smallest piglet nuzzled Kirsty and Rachel's legs before he went. "Thank you!" he squealed.

Rachel watched the pigs go. "What will happen to the goblin?" she asked. "He won't have to stay there forever, will he?"

Goldie's eyes twinkled mischievously. "Not forever, no," she said. "The dried mud will wash off as soon as it rains." She smiled cheerfully. "But Jack Frost won't be happy with him when he finds out we got the Sunshine Feather back!"

Twilight Magic

Now that the three friends were out of danger, Goldie expertly waved the Sunshine Feather. The sun began to set, just like it was supposed to. The girls watched as the sky turned orange, pink, and a deep red.

"Let's bring the Sunshine Feather back

to Doodle," Kirsty said. "And then we'd better go to bed!"

Rachel was yawning. "It's been another busy day, hasn't it?" She smiled.

As the sun set, the warmth quickly faded away. The girls soon found themselves shivering in their thin shirts. Goldie fluttered above them with the Sunshine Feather, waving it gently. A few sunbeams flooded onto Rachel and Kirsty's bare arms to keep them warm.

It was almost dark by the time they all got back to Kirsty's garden. They could just barely see the silhouette of Doodle on top of the barn roof.

Goldie flew up to give the rooster back his magic feather. As she did, Doodle came to life. His fiery feathers glowed brilliantly in the twilight. He turned to look at Rachel and Kirsty. "Will come —" he squawked urgently. But before he could say any more, the magic drained away. Doodle's colors faded and he became a rusty old weather vane again.

Every time the girls returned one of
Doodle's feathers, the rooster came to
life for a few seconds and squawked
a word or two. Rachel frowned as
she pieced together all the words that
Doodle had said so far. "Beware!
Jack Frost will come . . ." she
murmured. An icy shiver shot down
her spine, as if Jack Frost was already
there. "I think it's a warning, Kirsty.
Let's hope he doesn't come soon!"

Goldie looked worried. "Take
care of yourselves. And thank you for
everything," she said. She blew them a
stream of fairy kisses that sparkled in
the darkening sky. "I must go back
to Fairyland now. Good-bye!"

Kirsty and Rachel watched Goldie fly

away. Soon she was nothing more than a tiny golden speck in the distance. Then, just as the girls were about to get ready for bed, they heard footsteps. Mr. Tate came out of the house, looking around with a puzzled expression on his face. "Did I just hear a rooster crowing?" he asked.

"A rooster? At this time of day?" Kirsty replied innocently.

Mr. Tate frowned. "I must be hearing things," he said, turning to go back inside. "Good night, girls. Sleep well." He glanced up at Doodle as he headed back toward the house. "I'm sure that weather vane had a smaller tail before," he muttered, then shook his head. "Now I'm seeing things, too! It's definitely time to call it a night. . . ."

Kirsty and Rachel smiled at each other. "He's right!" Kirsty said. "Doodle *does* have four feathers now. We only have three more feathers to find. I wonder which one will be next!"

THE WEATHER FAIRIES

Crystal, Abigail, Pearl, and Goldie
all have their magic feathers back!
Now, can Rachel and Kirsty help

Evie the Mist Fairy?

Don't miss their next adventure!

RAINBOW magic™

There's Magic in Every Series!

The Rainbow Fairies

The Weather Fairies

The Jewel Fairies

The Pet Fairies

The Fun Day Fairies

The Petal Fairies

The Dance Fairies

Read them all!

SPECIAL EDITION

More Rainbow Magic Fun!
Three Stories in One!